ARCHITECT OF THE MOON

For my father

T.W.-J.

For P.A. and K.M.

I.W.

First paperback edition 1991
Second Printing 1995

Canadian Cataloguing in Publication Data

Wynne-Jones, Tim
Architect of the Moon

"A Meadow mouse paperback".
ISBN 0–88899–150–9

I. Wallace, Ian, 1950– . II. Title.

PS8595.Y6A7 1991 jC813′.54 C91–094796–1
PZ7.W96Ar 1991

Design by Michael Solomon
Printed and bound in Hong Kong by
Everbest Printing Co., Ltd.

A Meadow Mouse Paperback
Douglas & McIntyre
585 Bloor Street West
Toronto, Ontario M6G 1K5

ARCHITECT OF THE MOON

by Tim Wynne-Jones
pictures by Ian Wallace

A Meadow Mouse Paperback
Douglas & McIntyre
TORONTO/VANCOUVER

A message arrived from outer space,

SEPT

a message from the Moon.

Help! I'm falling apart. Yours, the Moon.

Luckily it arrived at the home
of brave block-builder
David Finebloom.

HELP!
I'M
FALLING
APART.
YOURS
THE MOON.

David waved from his window.
"Don't worry, Moon."

He gathered all the things he would need
for a busy night's work
and told his mum not to wait up.

Back in his room he laid out
a launch pad and turned the dial to Moon.
He activated his spaceship and

F
D

Whooosh! He was off.

6
F
5
4
3
1

He arrived just in time and

started right in. First the floor
of the tranquil sea,

then the valleys, hills and mountains.
He had brought all the right shapes and
all the right colors.

Bigger, bigger, bigger grew the Moon,
and rounder, too.
Course upon course, layer upon layer,
until

A
B
C
1
2
3
F
1954

it was done; it was full.
Hurray for David Finebloom!

It was a little rough in places,

but who on Earth would notice.

David waved from his spaceship.
"Don't worry, Mum!" He set the dial for
home and got there just in time for

STOCKERS
HOES
MOLNARS
MILK

breakfast on the porch.
A perfect five-minute egg.